CONTENTS

WHAT IS WEATHER?

We often talk about the weather, but what do we mean? Earth is surrounded by a blanket of gases. This blanket is called the atmosphere. Weather is just the current state of the atmosphere. The weather can change from day to day. It can even change from hour to hour! Different places have different weather. It can be clear where you live but stormy not far away.

We depend on the weather. Farmers need rain and sun to help their crops to grow. We can use the wind to make electricity. But weather can be harmful, too. Powerful storms damage houses and crops. Predicting the weather is important. It helps us to prepare for it.

WEATHER
AND SEASONS

QUESTIONS & ANSWERS

NANCY DICKMANN

Published in paperback in 2017 by
The Watts Publishing Group

Copyright © 2017 Brown Bear Books Ltd

All rights reserved.

For Brown Bear Books Ltd:
Text and Editor: Nancy Dickmann
Editorial Director: Lindsey Lowe
Children's Publisher: Anne O'Daly
Design Manager: Keith Davis
Designer and Illustrator: Supriya Sahai
Picture Manager: Sophie Mortimer

Concept development: Square and Circus/Brown Bear
Books Ltd

ISBN: 978 1 4451 5613 2

Printed in Malaysia

Franklin Watts
An imprint of
Hachette Children's Group
Part of the Watts Publishing Group
Carmelite House
50 Victoria Embankment
London EC4Y 0DZ

An Hachette UK company
www.hachette.co.uk
www.franklinwatts.co.uk

Picture Credits
All photographs copyright Shutterstock except page 12
Thinkstock.

Brown Bear Books has made every attempt to
contact the copyright holder. If you have any information
please contact licensing@brownbearbooks.co.uk

Websites
The website addresses (URLs) included in this book
were valid at the time of going to press. However,
it is possible that contents or addresses may change
following the publication of this book. No responsibility
for any such changes can be accepted by either the
author or the publisher.

CLIMATE

Weather is what happens over a short period of time. Climate is the average pattern of weather over many years. Some areas have a cool, damp climate.

CHANGING WEATHER

When weather changes it can cause problems. Droughts happen when an area gets less rain than usual for weeks or months. They can leave the ground dry and cracked.

WHAT ARE CLOUDS?

Look up at the sky. You will probably see at least one cloud. Clouds are made of water floating high in the sky. A cloud can be several kilometres across. It can hold as much water as a swimming pool! The water in clouds can fall to Earth. It can fall as rain, snow or hail.

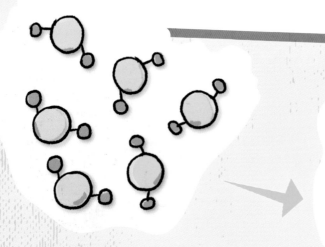

The atmosphere is full of water vapour. This is water in the form of a gas. It is made of tiny molecules that float in the air.

The air is also full of tiny dust particles.

6

A **cloud** forms when enough water droplets bunch together.

THE WATER CYCLE

All the water on Earth is recycled again and again. This is the water cycle. Water evaporates from the Earth's surface. It rises into the air to form clouds. Then it falls, and the cycle starts again.

More water droplets form and stick together.

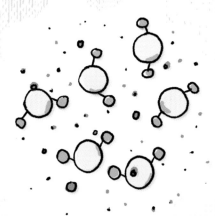

The water vapour and dust move around. They bump into each other. If the air is cool enough, the water and dust stick together. They make water droplets.

Some clouds are thick and puffy. Others are thin and wispy.

7

WHY DOES IT RAIN?

The water droplets inside a cloud start to stick together. They make bigger water droplets. These bigger droplets are heavy. If they get very heavy, they can't float in the air. They fall to Earth as precipitation.

There are several types of cloud. They have different shapes and bring different kinds of weather.

This is a lenticular cloud. It looks like a flying saucer!

Puffy white **cumulus** clouds form fairly low in the sky. They are common on sunny days, but can produce short showers.

Wispy cirrus clouds float high in the sky. They do not produce rain.

PRECIPITATION

Precipitation is any water that falls from the sky. It can be solid or liquid. Hail, snow, sleet and rain are all types of precipitation.

Huge **cumulonimbus** clouds send down hail and heavy rain. They also produce thunder and lightning.

Nimbostratus clouds are thick and grey. They form in flat layers. Steady rain or snow falls from these clouds.

WHY DO WE SEE RAINBOWS?

A rainbow is just a trick of the light. These colourful arches are sunlight bouncing off water! Sunlight looks white or colourless. But it is actually made up of all the colours mixed together. Conditions have to be just right for a rainbow to form. Water droplets in the air scatter the light. This shows us a rainbow of colours.

If you are lucky, you may see a double rainbow.

The Sun must be fairly low in the sky. The lower the Sun, the taller the rainbow will appear.

ROUND RAINBOWS?

Seeing the full circle of a rainbow is very rare. You must be above the water droplets that are making the rainbow. You might spot one from an aeroplane or the top of a mountain.

When sunlight passes through water, it bends and splits into different colours.

Water droplets

Sun's rays

To see a rainbow, the Sun must be behind you. There should be water droplets in front of you.

Rainbows look like arches. But they are actually circles. The horizon stops you from seeing the full circle.

11

ARE ALL SNOWFLAKES DIFFERENT?

Yes, they are! Water droplets in the air freeze when it gets cold. They form tiny ice crystals. The crystals bump into each other and stick together. When they get too heavy, they fall to the ground as snowflakes. Each flake can be made of hundreds of crystals. The crystals stick together in different ways. That gives each snowflake its own individual shape.

The warmer the air, the wetter the snow. Wet flakes are best for building snowmen.

Dendrite snowflakes form when the air is wet. They have six arms. The arms branch off into beautiful patterns.

Thin plate snowflakes form when the air is drier. They do not have arms.

SIX SIDES

Snowflakes are all different. But each one has a hexagonal (six-sided) shape. This is made by the shape of the water molecules. When they stick together, they make a six-sided shape.

This is a **sector plate** snowflake. It has a six-sided centre and six simple arms.

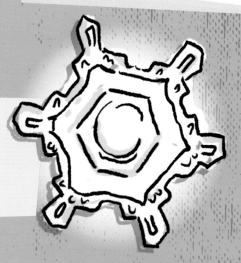

WHAT IS WIND?

Air is made up of tiny molecules. They move around and push outwards. This pushing force is called air pressure.

Some parts of the atmosphere have a lot of air molecules. This makes the air pressure high. Other places have fewer molecules. The air pressure there is low.

Air moves around to balance out the differences in pressure. Near the surface it moves from places with high pressure to places with low pressure. The moving air makes wind.

MEASURING WIND

We measure wind on the Beaufort Scale. It goes from zero to 12. Zero means calm air. Twelve is the strong winds in a hurricane.

A boat's sails catch the wind. The wind's force pushes the boat along.

The Sun heats the land. This heats the air directly above it.

As it rises, the air cools down. It becomes heavier so it starts to sink.

Air moves from high pressure to low pressure. This makes **wind**.

An area of **high pressure** forms along the ocean's surface.

Warm air rises. It leaves an area of **low pressure** beneath.

15

WHAT ARE SEASONS?

In most places, the weather changes during the year. Some months are cold and snowy. Other months are warm. We call these different times seasons. Many places have a pattern of four seasons that repeats each year.

Plants and animals change their behaviour with the seasons. More plants grow in the summer than in the winter. Some animals hibernate, or sleep, through the cold winters.

Many baby animals, such as lambs, are born in the spring.

DIFFERENT SEASONS
In some parts of the world, the temperature hardly changes during the year. These places have two seasons – rainy and dry.

In **spring,** the days get longer. The weather starts to warm up. Buds form on trees, and new plants grow.

THE FOUR SEASONS

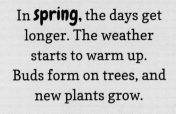

Winter is cold with short days. Few plants grow. Animals must find different things to eat.

In **summer,** it is hot. Days are long. There is plenty of food for animals. Plants grow quickly and trees are covered with leaves.

In the **autumn,** days get shorter. The weather starts to get cooler. Many tree leaves change colour and then fall off.

17

WHY ARE DAYS LONGER IN SUMMER?

An imaginary line called an axis runs through the Earth. It goes from the North Pole to the South Pole. The axis is tilted. This makes the Earth tilt or lean over as it moves around the Sun. The tilt is what causes the seasons. It takes a year for the Earth to make one trip around the Sun. That's why the seasons repeat each year.

AXIS

The Earth rotates on its axis every **24 hours**.

Earth's tilt means that in the winter, the Sun is lower in the sky.

NORTHERN HEMISPHERE

SUMMER
The northern half of the Earth tilts towards the Sun. This part gets more sunlight. The days are longer and the weather is hotter.

SPRING
The lean is sideways. The northern half isn't tilting towards or away from the Sun. The days start to get longer.

AUTUMN
The lean is sideways. The northern half isn't tilting towards or away from the Sun. The days start to get shorter.

WINTER
The northern half of the Earth tilts away from the Sun. This part gets less sunlight. Days are shorter and the weather is cold.

SOUTHERN HEMISPHERE

SOUTHERN SEASONS

When the northern part of the Earth leans towards the Sun, the southern half leans away. When it is summer in the north, it is winter in the south.

WHERE IS THE HOTTEST PLACE ON EARTH?

The highest temperature ever recorded was in Death Valley, USA. It reached 56.7 °C one day in 1913!

Scientists think that other places are hotter. They use satellites to measure temperatures. The satellites showed that the Lut Desert in Iran was much hotter.

The hottest place is actually inside the Earth. The planet's centre is thought to reach 6,650 °C!

A temperature of –89 °C was once recorded in Antarctica.

Death Valley, USA:
56.7 °C

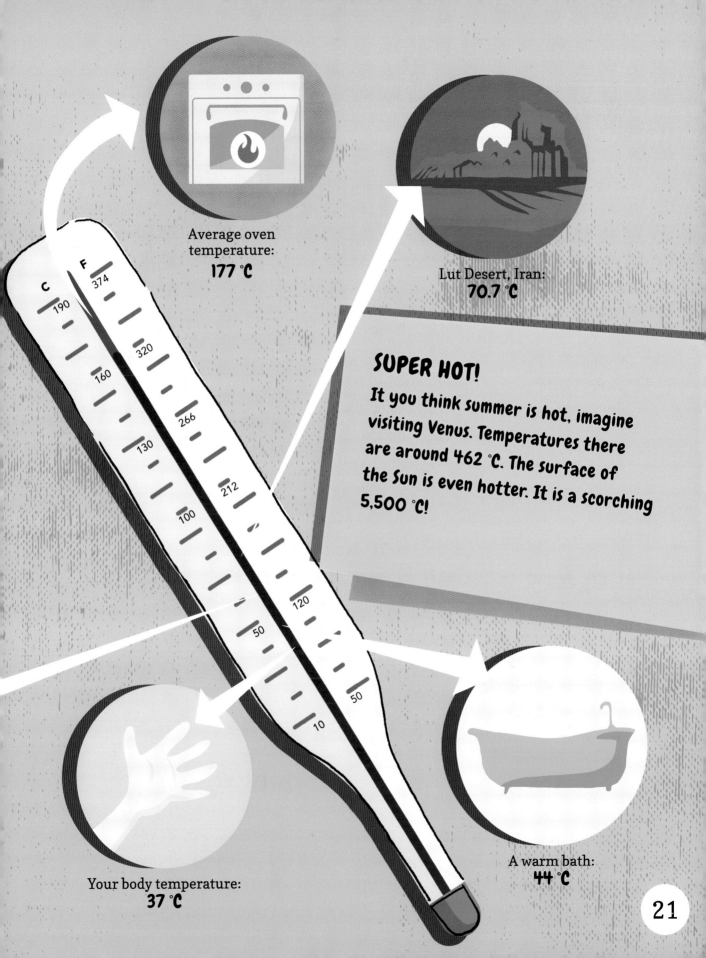

Average oven temperature:
177 ℃

Lut Desert, Iran:
70.7 ℃

SUPER HOT!
It you think summer is hot, imagine visiting Venus. Temperatures there are around 462 ℃. The surface of the Sun is even hotter. It is a scorching 5,500 ℃!

Your body temperature:
37 ℃

A warm bath:
44 ℃

WHAT IS EXTREME WEATHER?

Weather doesn't always follow the normal patterns. At times it gets pretty extreme! Droughts and heatwaves are types of extreme weather. Blizzards, tornadoes and flash floods are, too. Extreme weather is any event outside the normal pattern. It can cause a lot of damage.

HURRICANES

Hurricanes are powerful, swirling storms. They form over the ocean and move onto land. Hurricanes have strong winds and heavy rain. They are also called cyclones or typhoons.

Tornadoes also have strong winds, but they form over land.

INSIDE A HURRICANE

Near the top, **cooler air** moves out from the centre.

Warm, wet air rises quickly near the centre.

The **strongest winds** are just outside the eye. They blow at more than 119 km/h.

Heavy rains fall in thick bands. They surround the eye of the storm.

In the eye of the storm, it is **fairly calm.**

Winds blow near the surface. They push **warm, wet air** towards the centre.

HOW CAN I PREDICT THE WEATHER?

Meteorologists are scientists who measure the weather. They measure wind speed, temperature and air pressure. They get information from satellites in space. They use all this information to predict what the weather will be like. Even you can predict the weather with some simple tips!

If we can predict the weather, we can prepare for it.

AMAZING ANIMALS

Some animals can predict the weather. They sense changes in air pressure. The changes can mean a storm is coming. The animals find a safe place to shelter.

Is the **night sky** clear? In the winter, this can mean a cold day tomorrow.

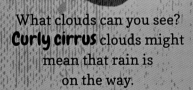

What clouds can you see? **Curly cirrus** clouds might mean that rain is on the way.

Are **birds** flying high in the sky? The weather is likely to be calm. Birds flying low can mean a storm is coming.

Is there **dew** on the grass? Dew after a dry night can mean a dry day ahead.

HOW DO WE USE WEATHER?

We use the weather every day. Farmers need sunshine and rain to help their crops to grow. Sailors use wind to push ships across the water. Wind once turned windmills to grind grain. Now we use wind to make electricity. Weather can be fun, too! We use snow for skiing and for snowball fights.

RAIN POWER

Rain keeps rivers full of water. The movement of fast-flowing rivers can make electricity. A dam has turbines in it. When a river flows through, it spins the turbines. That makes electricity.

Flying a kite is a fun way to use the wind.

Solar panels capture the energy in sunlight. They turn it into electricity.

Wind turbines spin as the wind blows. The spinning movement makes electricity.

Wires take the **electricity** where it is needed.

We use electricity in **houses**, schools and factories. It powers lights, computers and other things.

MAKE A WEATHER VANE

 Which way is the wind blowing?
Make this weather vane and use it to find out!

WHAT YOU NEED

* ruler, scissors, pencil and glue
* pen lid
* plastic bottle
* cardboard
* toothpicks
* cork
* sand
* knitting needle or wooden skewer

2 Put the pen lid halfway along one of the arrows. The open end of the lid should face down. Put the other arrow on top. Glue them together.

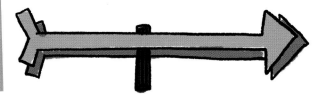

1 Draw an arrow 30 cm long on the cardboard. Cut it out. Then make another just the same.

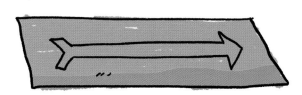

3 Make four labels: North, East, South and West. Stick each one to the end of a toothpick.

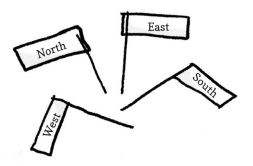

4 Push the toothpicks into the cork at right angles. The order is North, East, South and West.

5 Fill the bottle with sand to weigh it down.

Weather vanes have been used for hundreds of years.

6 Push the knitting needle into the cork. Balance the arrow on top.

USE YOUR WEATHER VANE

Take your weather vane outside. Use a compass to get the labels to point in the right directions. (An adult can help you.) When the wind blows, the arrow will change direction. It will point in the direction the wind is blowing.

GLOSSARY

air pressure weight of air pressing down on something

atmosphere layers of gases that surround the Earth

axis the imaginary rod that goes through the middle of Earth, from the North Pole to the South Pole

climate usual weather conditions in a particular region

crops plants that are grown by farmers for food or other uses

droplet very small drop of liquid

drought long period of time with very little or no rain

electricity form of energy that can be carried through wires and used to power machines and lights

evaporate turn from a liquid into a gas

hail small, round pieces of ice that fall from the sky

horizon line where the land or sea appears to meet the sky

hurricane large, powerful storm with very strong winds and heavy rain

ice crystal a shape formed when water freezes in a regular shape

meteorologist person whose job is measuring and predicting the weather

molecule smallest unit of a substance that has all the properties of that substance

particle very tiny piece of something

precipitation water that falls from the clouds to the ground

predict make an educated guess about something that will happen in the future

satellite machine that is sent into space to travel around the Earth

sleet mixture of rain and snow

temperature measurement of how hot or cold something is

tornado powerful, funnel-shaped storm with fast, spinning winds

turbine a machine with blades that spins when air or water moves past it

water vapour water that is in the form of gas

FURTHER RESOURCES

BOOKS

100 Facts Weather, Clare Oliver
(Miles Kelly, 2014)

Fact Cat Weather, Izzi Howell
(Wayland, 2016)

Project Geography Weather, Sally Hewitt
(Franklin Watts, 2013)

Science Corner Weather and Seasons, Alice Harman
(Wayland, 2014)

True or False? Weather, Daniel Nunn
(Raintree, 2013)

WEBSITES

www.bbc.co.uk/schools/whatisweather/
This BBC site has information about weather
and how it affects people.

www.metoffice.gov.uk/learning/weather-for-kids
Games and activities to help you find out more about
the weather and climate.

www.weatherforkids.org
Find out about different kinds of weather with
information, worksheets and quizzes.

INDEX